To my mother, who showed me the world

First published 2003
by Walker Books Ltd
87 Vauxhall Walk, London SE11 5HJ

This edition published 2004

1 2 3 4 5 6 7 8 9 10

This book has been typeset in Calligraphic Bold

Printed in China

British Library Cataloguing in Publication Data:
a catalogue record for this book is available from the British Library

ISBN 1-84428-489-1

www.walkerbooks.co.uk

THIS WALKER BOOK BELONGS TO:

Hello World

Michael Foreman

"Wake up, Baby. Let's go
and see the world."

"Listen, the birds are singing,
'Wake up, wake up.'"

"Hello, kittens. Come and see the world with us."

"Will there be trees to climb?"

"Yes, and much much more."

"Hello, puppies.
Come and see the world."
"Will there be fields to run in?"
"Yes, run along
with us."

“Hello, Mrs Frog. We're
off to see the world.”

*“Will there be a warm
rock to lie on?”*

“Yes, come and see.”

"Hello, Mrs
Duck. We're off
to see the world."

"Will there be a pond for me and my ducklings?"

"Yes, a pond and more besides."

"We'll waddle along with you, then."

"Hello, Mrs Hen.
Come with
us and see
the world."

“Will there be corn to peck?”

“Yes, come and bring
your chicks.”

"Follow us, follow us;
we're off to see the world."

And they saw a pond
with warm rocks to lie on.

And they saw
trees to climb.

And they saw fields of
flowers and stacks of corn.

And they loved it all.

"Is there more?"

"Yes, come and see."

When they reached the top
they sat and looked, and all the
wide world was before them.

And they looked up,

and saw the moon

And together they climbed the hill.

It was wonderful.

looking back at them.

and the stars